ENJOY THE RIDE

Teaching children through their own imagination

Written by DAVE DIGGLE
Illustrated by DANIEL JAMES DIGGLE

A Diggle de Doo production
www.digglededoo.com.au

First published 2006 by Diggle de Doo Australia
www.digglededoo.com.au

© Diggle de Doo Productions Pty Ltd 2006

National Library of Australia
Cataloguing-in-Publication Entry

Diggle, Dave.
Enjoy the ride.

For primary school children.
ISBN 0 9775104 0 9.

I. Diggle, Daniel James. II. Title.
A823.4

Teaching children through their own imagination

Why use metaphors?

Metaphors are stories in which one object is likened to another. This can be used to create a meaningful connection between the message being delivered and one's own personal experience.

One of our greatest attributes when we are young is our unrestricted imagination. A world of endless possibilities is ours to explore.

It is with this imagination that we become our own super heroes, fighting evil and feeling confident, safe and untouchable – no matter what the reality of our circumstances are at the time.

For some of us it is pure, unbridled imagination. For others, it is an escape from undesirable circumstances.

The difference between an adult and child's coping mechanism is that adults place deductive logic on situations based on many years of experience, attempting to justify and reason with issues within the boundaries of conscious logic.

As children do not have the benefit of so many years of experience, they tend to look for a safe alternative to control the situation in their own way. A child's spirit of adventure will always find their own happy ending no matter how far fetched it may appear.

Inspire, motivate, support, guide, cherish and nurture. These are all things we want to do for children – and never more so than when we have a child with a problem.

A simple, elegant way to deal with many of these childhood issues is through the use of metaphor. A well constructed metaphor offers a non-confronting alternate solution to an issue by passively guiding the child through a story to find their own conclusions.

Metaphor brings imagination to life. The key to the metaphors in this collection is that one story can captivate so many imaginations simultaneously. The stories are abstract to the level where children create their personal connections to the story and they attribute their own meanings and therefore, take control and come to their own solutions.

This book is a collection of metaphors helping children deal with some common issues. These metaphors are designed for an adult to read to a child and combine bright vibrant illustrations with the use of specific language patterns weaved throughout to draw the adult and child in and be part of the adventure.

People are always searching for their own answers. As they search, they attribute their own meaning to things and children are no different.

As you read each story, in the child's mind associations are created to the story's message. Each metaphor gently guides the child through an adventure with the characters, opening up new possibilities for the them and leads them to a desirable conclusion. Subconsciously, the mind processes and creates its own individual solution.

So hop in and enjoy the ride as we teach our children through their own imagination...

Table of Contents

Ewan

Ewan is a nine year old little boy with red hair, a freckly face, big smile and thick glasses. He loves to read his comic books at night by flash light under his covers, often dreaming of being a super hero and saving the world. He would imagine his red hair was like a fireball; his glasses enabled him to see through walls; and his freckly face – well that just made him cute!

Ewan had just moved into a new house with his Mum, Dad and Roger. Roger is his old shaggy dog who sleeps at the end of his bed. Their new house overlooks a big park with a pond, ducks, geese and plenty of space to run around and chase a ball with Roger.

Although Ewan is a very bright little boy he hated going to school, not because he didn't like school - his school is a fantastic old building with big stain glass windows and arches into every class room. Ewan hated going to school because some of the kids in his class tease him about his glasses, his red hair and even his cute freckly face.

They call him names like 'four-eyes' or 'nerd', which makes some of the other children in the class laugh at Ewan too. This makes him very upset and a little bit annoyed.

For now, Ewan doesn't have to worry about that as it is the first day of his summer holidays and he has a new house, garden and park to explore with his best friend Roger.

As the weeks go by, Ewan and Roger explore the house, the garden, the park and even the neighbour's garden. However, there was still one place left to explore, a place he was told he couldn't go. One place where Ewan hadn't dared to go… the attic!

Ewan decided today was the day! He took the big old brass key from the downstairs key rack and held it in his hands. Ewan felt a little nervous but he just knew he had to explore. After all, that's what super heroes do!

As Ewan opened the creaky old door, there was a tiny light coming through the small window way up high at the end of the attic. It wasn't enough light to see where he was going, so he switched on his flash light. Ewan didn't know what he was going to find.

As his eyes adjusted to the dimly lit room there didn't appear to be too much to see at first, just some old books, old clothes and a wooden chest that was covered in dust.

Ewan shone his flashlight all around the dark, dusty attic finally stopping on the old wooden chest. With curious excitement, Ewan walked over and cautiously opened it. The chest creaked and groaned with old age as the big wooden top finally came to rest on it's hinges. Inside was a smaller box almost identical to that which it was in.

On the front of the smaller box was a mirror. Ewan wiped away the dust, seeing himself in the small mirror, almost looking back at himself. Below the mirror was also a plaque that read:

Only you can open this chest

Ewan sat and thought. He didn't know if he should open it. He wanted to, it felt right and Ewan could see himself, so that must mean it was meant for him.

"After all, who was the message for if not for me?" Ewan said to himself, although he was a little scared of what he may find.

Ewan decided to open the old dusty box very slowly. Inside was covered in soft red velvet and sitting on the velvet was an envelope. He carefully took the envelope out of the box and looked inside. Inside the envelope was a card… and a small ring!

Excitedly, Ewan picked up the ring. It was like glass… like you could see right through it - it looked almost invisible. Ewan slipped the ring on his finger… fitting perfectly.

5

He then picked up the card. There was a lot of writing on it so he just read the first lines. The card read:

Instruction for the Magic Shield. Place this ring on your finger - you now have the power.

"Wow! This is just like real super hero stuff!" exclaimed Ewan to himself. He felt very excited.

Ewan was so excited that he couldn't sleep that night. He thought about what the card had said to him. He lay awake looking at the ring as it glowed on his bedside table.

"I can't wait to try the magic ring," Ewan whispered to himself. On what, he wasn't too sure. He still didn't realise just how powerful the ring is.

The next morning Ewan rushed to school very excited about trying his new magic shield. He didn't really know what this shield was used for. "I wonder what it will do?" thought Ewan. "What will it shield me against and how do I use it?" He clutched the ring in his pocket and twisted it between his fingers, feeling the warm glow.

As he walked through the big iron gates into the school playground two older boys who usually tease Ewan started to walk towards him. "Not again!" thought Ewan. These two boys had been bullying him all year.

The boys started calling Ewan names and laughing at him.

"Four eyes!" said one of the boys as he laughed at Ewan.

"Carrot top!" said the other.

"Very original," thought Ewan to himself. "They are the same names they have been calling me all year. You would think they could have come up with some new ones over the holidays." Ewan carried on walking as the boys followed him.

"Now, let's see what this shield can actually do," thought Ewan, a little unsure. "I guess right now is the best time to start," he said to himself as he slipped the magic ring on his finger.

He instantly started to feel happier, stronger and more confident. He noticed with delight the voices of the two boys starting to become softer… and softer… and softer, until he couldn't hear them at all anymore.

He could still hear the other, more important noises such as the children playing in the playground and the school bell ringing for class to start. He could even hear cars passing on the road outside the school… but he couldn't hear the two bullies. It was like their voices had been turned down with a TV remote control. They looked very silly with their mouths moving but no sound coming out!

Ewan smiled as he walked past the two boys and into class, taking the ring off as he sat at his desk.

"This is great!" thought Ewan, "I really do have the power. I am a super hero!"

The children were waiting in their class for their teacher to arrive. Some were chatting about what they had done during the school holidays and others were shouting across the class or throwing paper airplanes.

Suddenly, a boy at the front of the room who was teasing a girl stopped and looked at Ewan. He started calling Ewan names, "Oi nerd," he said, "What you looking at?"

Ewan reached into his pocket and once again placed the ring on his finger. Instantly the boy's voice began fading until Ewan couldn't hear him anymore. Sure, his lips were still moving but Ewan didn't hear a word the boy was saying. Ewan could still hear all the shouting and excitement in the class but not the bully.

"I do have the power," said Ewan. Ewan smiled to himself and the bully walked away with a confused look on his face. No one had ever ignored the bully before.

Ewan now had the power to turn off the voices from those who were teasing him, simply with a magic shield controlled by Ewan's mind and this very special ring that nobody else could see.

"This is the best thing ever!" said Ewan excitedly to himself. "I must rush home and charge the ring so it will shield me tomorrow."

As the home-time bell sounded, Ewan ran as fast as he could out of the classroom, across the playground, over the football field, down the lane, into his street, jumping the front gate outside his home. He burst through the kitchen door rushing past his Mum and up to his bedroom, slamming the door behind him.

Safely inside his room, Ewan pulled the small wooden box out from under his bed. He looked into the mirror on the front and smiled before getting the card out of the box with the instructions on it.

Ewan placed the box on the floor at the end of his bed and sat down with the ring and instructions in his hand. He read the card:

You must take care of the Magic Shield by charging this ring. Charge it each night and place it back in the box. It is your responsibility now.

Holding the ring in the palm of his hand he read the rest of the card out loud:

Now... close your eyes and imagine a happy time... a very special and happy time... one where you are so happy that you cannot stop smiling. Now... imagine that time where your whole body felt like it was smiling and laughing with you.

Ewan's magic ring began to glow in the palm of his hand. It was getting warmer as it recharged, the more Ewan smiled the brighter and hotter the ring became. Ewan smiled so much he began to laugh and the ring became even brighter, almost lighting up his bedroom.

Ewan's sides ached from all the laughing and his face tingled from all the smiling so he placed the ring back into the box ready for the next day. He climbed into bed, pulled the sheets over his head and turned on his torch.

He began to read his comic book, realising that he is just as strong as any super hero. He didn't read about the super hero that night. Instead, he imagined it was him on the pages fighting crime, rescuing people and having all that power.

Ewan doesn't get teased anymore at school. You may think it's because of the magic shield – but it is because of Ewan.

The bullies got bored with teasing somebody who didn't hear what they had to say and ignored their childish name calling. Ewan didn't hear them, he just smiled and walked away taking their energy away from them just like a super hero would.

Ewan still carries his magic shield everywhere he goes and charges it every night just in case… but I don't think he will ever need it again – do you?

Mary

Mary is a bright yellow canary who lives with her Mum and Dad in a tall tree in an African rainforest.

Mary's home overhangs a very nice part of the river bank estate with lovely neighbours, good friends and a very beautiful nest to live in. Mary even has her own room that she helped her dad decorate with local leaves, moss and twigs.

Mary's Dad works for a mining company so he isn't always home, he works very long hours, sometimes all night long.

When he is home, Mary and her Dad play together for hours on the branches outside their nest. They sometimes play late into the night and occasionally even miss dinner.

One windy day, Mary was playing in her nest. She had been playing there all morning and was getting rather bored, so she decided to go and play outside on the branches - it was more fun out there and besides, it is where she and her Dad always played together.

Mary knew she wasn't allowed to play outside without her Mum or Dad being with her, she had been told many times.

Mary slowly edged herself out of the nest and out on to the branch, "This isn't so dangerous," said Mary to herself, but you could hear the nervousness in her voice.

One step at a time she climbed out further… and further until there was only the river below her and it was a very long drop. "It's a long way down," said Mary timidly to herself still clutching the thin branches.

Just as Mary started to feel a little more confident, a strong gust of wind blew past her, blowing her out of the tree and the safety of the nest!

Mary drifted gently down past all the branches with her wings stretched out as wide as she could make them. She didn't know how to fly yet, she was too young, but had seen her Mum and Dad fly many times. Splash! Mary landed in the river.

The landing was very gentle but she still went under the water. She got water up her nose and into her beak.

"Help! Help I can't swim!" cried Mary as her head briefly rose above the water. She was very scared and was kicking her little feet as hard as she could, trying very hard to stay afloat.

The river gently carried her away from her home and the safety of her Mum and Dad, "Help Mum, Dad… can you hear me?" Mary shouted at the top of her voice.

Mary knew no one had noticed her fall from the branch. After all, no one knew she was out there where she shouldn't have been playing alone.

Mary managed to slowly float over to the river bank by clinging onto small rocks under the water with her claws. She stretched her neck and pointed just the tip of her beak above the water.

Once on the river bank she lay there cold and wet, trying to catch her breath, "Why didn't I listen to Mum and Dad and just stay where it is safe?" she thought to herself, frantically looking around for a way to get home.

Mary didn't recognise anything, she knew she was very lost and felt very scared.

Suddenly, a voice came from within the tall grass on the edge of the river, "The name's Python… Sly Python" said the voice. It was a soft, smooth and gentle voice. It almost sounded slippery. Mary was just so relieved to hear someone who may be able to help her get home.

"My name is Mary and I'm lost. Could you help me get home?" asked Mary, getting a little teary at the thought of going to the safety of her home and being with her Mum and Dad again.

"Of course I can," said Sly, "You can trust me - I'm a snake!"

Sly was long and thin. He circled her, slowly sniffing her with his forked tongue, appearing to be checking her out from beak to feet with each dart. This made Mary feel very nervous.

Mary looked at Sly and remembered what her Mum and Dad had said to her about stranger danger.

Mary felt uneasy inside at the thought of trusting Sly Python. In fact, the more he began to slither himself around and around Mary, he got closer and closer. And the closer he got to Mary, the more uncomfortable she began to feel.

"Umm… I don't think I should be asking you for help Mr Python. My Mum and Dad have always told me not to talk to people I don't know," said Mary very nervously, as his tail coiled her muddy feet. "And I have never met you before… I'm sure you are a nice snake but I had better be on my way now."

With that, Mary jumped out of the very tight grip Sly Python had on her and ran away as fast as her little legs would go.

"Bother!" said Sly Python as he slithered away into the tall grass looking for his next lunch date.

"That was too close," said Mary to herself, feeling very lucky to have not ended up as lunch for the slithering python. Mary started to make her way back up river looking for her Mum and Dad.

Suddenly another voice made her jump, "Would you like a ride?" the deep voice asked.

Mary looked around but couldn't see anyone, "Who said that?" asked Mary shakily as she hid behind a tree.

Just then a big splash, a loud crash and there on the river bank was an alligator!

He was huge, the size of a fallen tree but with shiny long white teeth for all to see.

"I'm Mr Alligator, but you can call me Al. You look lost. Can I offer you a ride home?"

"Do you know my Mum and Dad then?" asked Mary very excited.

"Aahh of course I do", he said with his big alligator smile, "They asked me to come

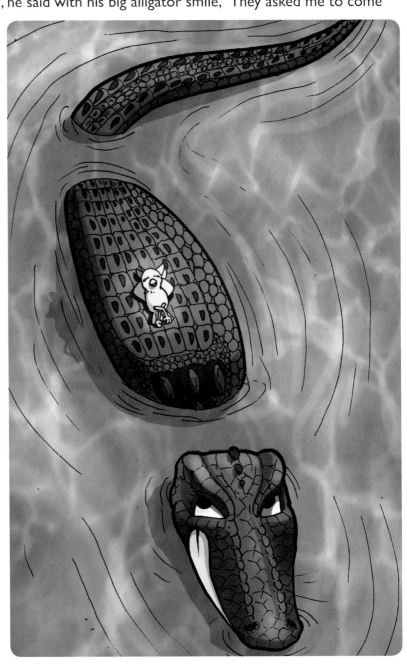

and collect you from school." Al was obviously making it all up as Mary wasn't at school today.

But Mary didn't notice and with the thought of going home in Mary's mind, she slowly climbed on the back of the Alligator.

"Are you sure you know where my home is, Mr Alligator?"

Al smiled a cheeky alligator smile to himself as he slipped back into the river with Mary perched firmly on his back. He made his way to the centre of the wide river with only his snout and Mary sticking out of the water. Just as they reached the middle, he suddenly stopped.

"Yum, yum lunch time!" he shouted lifting himself high out of the water and trying to get the little yellow canary from his back with his snapping teeth.

With a flick of his large tail, Mary was launched into the air heading for the very sharp end of the alligator.

"You don't know my Mum and Dad at all!" yelped Mary in her loudest voice as she rebounded off the top of Al's head.

Kicking her legs and flapping her wings she aimed for the safety of the river bank, reaching out with all her strength and concentration.

She was about to land back in the deep, dark murky water. She could see it getting closer and closer. As she closed her eyes and braced herself for the cold water, she felt a cool breeze under her wings. She was actually flying - she was no longer falling, but gliding!

Mary flew well enough to make it back to the edge of the river. It wasn't graceful but she made it, landing beak first pushing dirt up her nose.

Mary jumped up as fast as she could and looked back at the river wide-eyed, looking fearfully for the hungry alligator's snout and white teeth.

There was nothing to be seen but a calm river gently flowing with no sign that Al the Alligator had ever been there - but you knew he was there somewhere.

Mary frantically scrambled to the middle of a grassy verge. She moved far enough away from the river bank in case the Alligator was close and far enough away from the long grass to be safe from the slippery python.

Mary began to cry. She was lost, cold and alone. She covered her eyes with her dripping wet wings and started to think about her Mum and Dad, wondering if they had realised she was actually missing. Mary missed them… she missed them so much.

"I now know why they didn't want me to play outside on my own," said Mary while wiping a tear from her eye, "I wish I was home right now."

Just then the sky appeared to get darker, like a large shadow had blocked out the sun. Mary looked up wondering what was happening. She could see something moving above her.

Mary shielded her eyes from the bright sunlight trying to make out what was soaring so high in the sky… almost hypnotising her… making her concentrate on it's magnificent grace.

The shadow disappeared in a flash - as fast as the click of your fingers! Only the bright sunlight was visible again making Mary squint even more.

"Are you Mary Canary?" asked a deep voice from behind her.

"Yes, yes I am. Are you going to try to eat me too?" Mary cowered down into a small fluffy ball lifting one wing to protect herself, scared of what may happen next.

"Ha! Ha! No, I'm Sergeant Ernest Eagle. I am a policeman. I have been looking for you all afternoon. Your Mum and Dad are very upset and I am sure they will be very pleased to see you home safe and sound.

Ernest bent down next to Mary and placed his strong wing on Mary's shoulder to reassure her she was safe.

"If you look just across the river you can see your home," said Sergeant Ernest in his deep but comforting voice.

"I didn't realise I was so close to home," said Mary with a puzzled look on her face.

"It felt like I was so very far away, so far I thought I would never find my way back. But I was here all the time."

Again the Sergeant laughed, "You don't have to go too far from home to feel lost," he said earnestly.

"I will never leave the nest without telling Mum or Dad again," said Mary, "NEVER!"

Melanie

It was Melanie Wellington's first day at Pilot school. She was very nervous and didn't know any of the other young whales in her class. Melanie was following in the great Wellington family tradition of pilots. Her grandfather was a great pilot - some say the greatest pilot there ever was.

In Melanie's class there were pictures of all the greatest whales that ever piloted and in the middle of all the pictures were two Wellingtons: Melanie's father and grandfather!

Although it was Melanie's family, she felt very intimidated, "I could never be as good a pilot as my dad," said Melanie to herself.

Melanie wanted to be a pilot whale just like her father and grandfather. Melanie loved her dad and he was the best pilot whale she knew. She would often swim up front with him as he guided the pod through the Pacific Ocean from Tenerife to the tip of Australia without ever getting lost and always knowing the best seafood shops on the way.

Melanie studied hard as it's not like on land where there are street signs or street maps. Under water the whales have to rely on navigation by currents, rock formations and an inbuilt natural compass.

After several months, Melanie felt a little more confident but her big end of year exam was coming up and the entire class of young pilots-in-training were nervous.

Mickey Whale, one of the boys in Melanie's class, said it was unfair as Melanie must know more than the rest of them. After all, her dad was one of the greatest pilots. Melanie was starting to feel the pressure. As if Mickey wasn't bad enough, Melanie's own father was testing her on her navigation every time they would go out to the shops or to a restaurant for calamari and chips.

Melanie knew she had to do well in her end of year exams. "What am I going to do?" exclaimed Melanie, "What if I fail the exam? All the other whales will laugh at me and worse than that - my father will be so disappointed in me."

As Melanie lay on her waterbed worrying about tomorrow's exam, she suddenly had a thought, "I know! I will write the answers to the questions on the under side of my fin and if I get stuck I can just take a quick look."

So Melanie set about writing the answers to all the exam questions on the underside of her fin.

The next day Melanie breezed through the exam finishing first, way ahead of all the other whales. She rushed out of the exam room with a big sigh of relief, quickly rubbing the answers off her fin on a kelp bed before anyone could see.

That afternoon every whale that was any whale was at the Pilot Graduation Ceremony held at the Hanging Rock Stadium.

"And this year's top graduate with a perfect score of 100% is Melanie Wellington!" read the principal of the school, Ms Orca.

All the whales cheered and flapped and Melanie's Mum and Dad looked so proud. Melanie started to feel a little guilty as Humphrey Humpington should have been the top graduate - he got 97%. Rather than Melanie owning up to her cheating she swam up onto stage and accepted her Pilot Fins as she posed for the local photographers from the *Daily Echo* newspaper.

Melanie's father announced that due to a barnacle on his nose which Dr Crab was going to remove, he couldn't escort the graduates to the east coast for schoolies this year. However, in light of Melanie's great results in her end of year exam he was going to let Melanie pilot the graduates on her own.

This was a big honor for Melanie, as all the whales' parents trusted Mr Wellington with their young whales. He had guided the graduates every year for the past ten years as did his father before that.

Melanie rushed home, quickly packing a sea chest for her exciting trip.

"Now Melanie," said her father, "Are you sure you can do this?"

"Dad!" said Melanie, "I'm the best whale in the class, the big fish now, so of course I can do it."

With that Melanie rushed off, picking up the other graduates on her way. It wasn't long before they were off on their first ever adventure with Melanie at the front as head Pilot, just like her father and his father before him.

After about twelve hours of swimming, Melanie stopped for a rest.

"Are we there yet?" asked Humphrey. By his calculations they should have been there three hours ago.

Melanie looked around for some familiar signs of the east coast, but nothing. She smiled nervously, "You must be wrong Humphrey," said Melanie, "I know what I am doing, I got 100% remember."

"Well, how long before we get there?" asked Mickey, "I'm starving, tired and my fin has a blister."

"We can't be too far," said Melanie, "I will just surface and check."

With that Melanie swam to the surface looking for their destination. Melanie surfaced again and again but nothing. She couldn't even see any land at all. They were lost.

Melanie started to panic, "What will I do? What will I say to the others?" Melanie went back to the pod to tell them the bad news.

"Umm… we are a little off course," said Melanie, "But don't worry, I got 100% in navigation so I will get us there! Let's go this way, no let's go this way, or is it this way?"

The class was completely lost!

"What are we going to do?" asked Mazy, the southern right whale, "You're the Pilot, you must get us there!"

Melanie started to get scared, "I wish I had listened better in class instead of cheating," said Melanie to herself. It was starting to get dark, the whales were a long way from home - cold, hungry and they had no idea what to do next.

"We are very lost," said Humphrey, "And it's your fault Melanie."

Melanie knew Humphrey was right. It was her responsibility to get the whales to their destination and she had failed.

Just then Mickey exclaimed, "I can see something coming!"

"Where?" asked Melanie.

"Look deep, deep down. There, it's coming towards us." It was getting bigger and bigger and clearer and clearer.

"It's Mr Wellington!" said Mazy.

"You didn't think I would let you go off on your first trip without a parent to watch over you, did you?" said Mr Wellington.

Melanie was so happy to see her Dad, she flung herself at him and cried, "I'm sorry Dad I should have never cheated. I will never ever do it again."

"Your Mum and I suspected you had cheated," said Mr Wellington, "Even your Grandfather needed to study in order to become the greatest pilot."

Mr Wellington escorted the graduates to schoolies, before taking Melanie home where she spent all summer studying and she really did study.

Melanie sat her exams again at the end of the summer and passed and this time earned her pilots fins. She didn't get 100% and maybe she isn't as good a pilot as her father or grandfather yet, but with some practise and guidance from Dad she will be.

Brian

Brian was like most other little boys: he loved to play with his playstation, watch his favourite TV shows and his favourite thing of all was eating junk food!

He would love to sit and chomp on chips while watching a cartoon, or sip on a fizzy drink while slouching in his bean bag with his game boy.

Brian would have chocolate on toast for breakfast, a chip sandwich for lunch and a burger for dinner and always finished off with dessert - not to mention the sweets in-between.

One morning Brian woke to the sound of his alarm clock, "Oh no, time for school again," mumbled Brain with a globule of dribble still on his cheek.

He climbed out of bed and shuffled his way to the bathroom to …."Now what am I supposed to do in here?" said Brian to himself a little confused, as he scratched his head through his sticky-up bed-head.

"Oh well, it couldn't have been that important I suppose, I will go and get ready for school," he said, almost forgetting that it had ever happened.

As Brian walked out of the bathroom he stood in the hallway looking up and down the narrow corridor. He stared at the photos that hung along the floral wallpaper with a puzzled look on his face.

"Where is my bedroom?" said Brian to himself, as he scratched his bottom and stuck a finger in his ear to give it a wiggle.

"I must be tired," he thought, as he pulled his pyjamas up a little to cover his bottom again.

Brian's Mum appeared and hurried him into his room guiding him by his shoulders as she pushed him from behind, moving a lot faster than Brian liked to travel at that time of morning.

Once in the bedroom she pointed to where she had set out his clothes on the end of his bed.

"Come on Brian, you will be late for school again if you don't get a move on," she said as she rushed out again looking for Brian's sister who was already up, showered and on her way downstairs to eat breakfast.

Brian sat on the end of his bed for a minute or two staring at his pile of clothes before he began to get dressed.

When he got down to his shoes, Brian stopped. He sat and looked at the shoes as though examining them for the first time, but he just couldn't remember which shoe went on which foot.

He shook his head, trying to shake his memory up a little. Nothing came to mind,

so Brian just put them on the first foot that came to hand. He tucked the laces into the sides of the shoes, not bothering to tie them up.

Brian made his way down to the kitchen, finding his way by smelling the toast cooking under the grill. He grabbed his breakfast and rushed out to the car, ready for school.

He leaned against the car, munching on the chocolate smothered toast, trying to get it all in his mouth as fast as he could before it melted over the edges and down his fingers.

Brian looked in the car wing mirror and could see his reflection. He noticed he had chocolate from one side of his face to the other. "Oh no," he thought.

Using his tongue, he carefully removed each morsel with pin-point accuracy. He smiled to himself, satisfied that he hadn't wasted any.

After a while, Brian's Mum looked out of the kitchen window with a confused look on her face, wondering why Brian was standing next to the car. "Brian," she shouted at the top of her voice out of the open window, "You will miss your bus if you don't hurry."

Brian, feeling a little bewildered, stumbled out to the bus stop which was right outside the front gate of his house. He waited while two buses drove past him, until another kid arrived with the same school uniform he was wearing. He then followed her to school; he thought that was the safest option.

Brian was beginning to worry, "Why can't I remember things?" he wondered as he looked out of the bus window.

"Maybe I'm sick? Nah, I feel fine," he thought as he felt his forehead, almost trying to convince himself everything was ok.

Brian got off the bus with the girl and followed her into school. She was a year or two older than Brian and was becoming a little concerned by the boy who was following her everywhere. She kept looking over her shoulder at Brian, who carried on walking behind her with his hands in his pockets and laces now flapping in the breeze.

Brian sat down at the desk still not knowing why he could not remember the things he did every day.

"I think you're in the wrong class," boomed a deep voice from the front. The teacher had come in and Brian was indeed sitting in the wrong class - he had followed the older girl into her classroom.

The class erupted into a cheer as the teacher took Brian to his classroom, but not before helping him change his shoes over as the left was still on the right foot and the right was still on the left foot.

Brian had a terrible day at school, forgetting how to do maths and not being able to spell the simplest of words. Finally three o'clock arrived and the bell rang - it was time to go home.

Brian breathed a deep sigh of relief and looked around for the same girl to follow home on the bus, this time keeping his distance.

He went to bed early that night thinking a good night's sleep would help him feel better, but not until he finished his burger and chips for dinner and ice-cream for dessert.

Brian climbed into bed and switched out the light. He slipped deeper and deeper into a comfortable and relaxing sleep.

"Excuse me, excuse me I would like a word with you!"

Brian woke with a start and switched on his bedside light, but there was no one in the room, or so he thought. .

"Ah… it must have been a dream," chuckled Brian to himself and lay back down again, wondering if the second helping of ice cream had been too much.

"Excuse me, I want to talk to YOU!" Again Brian sat bolt upright! This time he knew it wasn't a dream, he hadn't gone back to sleep yet.

"Who's there?" asked Brain in a nervous, although demanding voice.

"My name is Nigel, Nigel Nerd. This is Lenny Logic and back there is Felicity History," said the voice calmly.

"We are your brain managers: we help you think and remember by searching your brain for the right things for you to say and do," said the voice again.

Brian was still looking around the room for the source of the voice, hanging over the edge of his bed, looking under it amongst all the old toys and dust.

"Well you guys didn't do a very good job today, did you? I mean, I had a terrible day," said Brian as he picked up his bedside lamp trying to shine some light on the problem.

"Well you can't blame us for that, we have decided to go out on strike!" said Lenny defiantly. "We refuse to work anymore until you take better care of yourself and us here in your body."

"Why should I?" asked Brian feeling a little braver now, "Isn't it your job to help me? Anyway, how exactly do you do that?"

"Yes, it is our job. Every time you do something, we file it away in your brain for the next time you need it, like a library files books," explained Lenny very logically.

"Because you eat so much junk food, we in your brain don't get fed properly. We need proper food with healthy things in it," said Felicity in her most motherly voice.

"We need good healthy food to get through to us to help give us enough energy. There is a lot to keep in order here in your brain," said Nigel.

"We are working on nothing but junk food and we don't want to do that anymore. If you want us to start working properly again, you will have to start feeding us properly with good foods that give us energy," said Felicity in her strongest of strong voices.

Brian laughed out loud, "That's silly, you are only voices in my head and I don't really need you, do I?" He turned out his light before going to sleep, covering his head with his blankets in an attempt to keep the managers' voices out.

The next morning Brain woke with a start. He lay and thought about the night before, "I had the strangest dream last night," he said aloud as he rubbed his head, feeling tired.

Brian was so slow and groggy. He couldn't tie his shoes again, couldn't remember where his school books were and was running so late his Mum decided to drive him to school. She even walked him to his class, just in case there was a repeat of yesterday.

Brian's day went from bad to worse. He forgot his homework assignment, then lost his class on a trip to the local zoo and missed his bus home.

"It's getting worse," thought Brian, "There are so many things I have forgotten today and that's only the things I can remember that I have forgotten." As Brian walked home he started to think about the dream he had had the night before.

Brian walked straight past his gate, only remembering to stop when his Mum shouted at him from the kitchen window. He was late for dinner!

That night as Brian lay down on his bed he began to worry. He wasn't too sure what he was worried about as he had forgotten what he had been worrying over.

"You need to help yourself," said a voice from deep inside. It was a voice which made Brian relax, a comforting voice like your own.

"Listen to me carefully; I know what your body needs. I can help you with your problems, it's my job," said Nigel's voice, "I have the answers you are looking for."

"I can help you tie your shoes," said Lenny.

"And I can help you remember where your class is and what bus to take to school," said Felicity in her know-it-all voice she saved for times when she could say, "I told you so."

"But I like junk food," said Brian defiantly. "Besides everyone else eats it, don't they?"

"You don't have to stop it all together," said Lenny, "You just need to eat more healthy stuff too, otherwise other parts of your body will start to go out on strike and they don't always warn you, like I'm telling you now."

Brian lay there with his hands over his eyes, trying to think of a clever answer to his problem but was having trouble remembering why he liked the junk food in the first place.

"I know, I know," said Brian, "I understand I need to take better care of myself. I am getting a little chubby and I do get out of breath when I run."

Brian thought back to his gym class last week. He was the last one out of the change room and the last one to finish the school cross-country run.

"I do need to eat better foods like vegetables and fruit and slow down on the junk food and I know I can do it if I want to - and I really do want to," thought Brian. Nigel, Lenny and Felicity were listening to every word Brian was thinking.

Felicity smiled, "That's right and you do."

"You will start to remember things easily now, and be able to do the little things like tie your shoes and clean your teeth without thinking." said Lenny Logic excited about getting back to work.

Nigel grabbed his books again, "You will be able to solve all those maths questions and spelling tests. We will work together to make each day easier and easier," said Nigel in a nerdy sort of way.

"That's what we do, we work together," said Brian almost convinced.

Brian knew he had to make the change from junk food to fruit and from unhealthy to healthy and now was the time as he had forgotten all his old habits.

Two weeks later Brian came rushing into the kitchen after school, "Mum, Mum look I got 100% on my spelling test."

"Well done Brian!" said his Mum with a big smile on her face, "I'm so proud of you."

"Thanks guys," whispered Brian to himself as he sank his teeth into a nice juicy red apple.

"No… thank you" whispered Nigel.

TEST RESULTS
STUDENT: BRIAN
10
A

Sammy

On the outskirts of town is a big forest. The forest is lush and green and has many different types of trees, flowers and animals. It stretches for miles and miles as far as the eye can see and it is a magnificent sight.

Deep, deep, deep down in the heart of this forest is a clearing. An area where the sun shines through onto the big oak tree's leaves, making them shiny and warm. And as the breeze blows the branches sway gently from side to side.

No one knows just how old the great oak tree is but everyone agrees he is the wisest of all the trees in the forest. Next to the great oak is a beautiful willow tree with her long branches hanging down almost to the ground.

If you stop, watch and listen very hard you can feel, see and hear her dancing to the whistling tune of the wind like a ballerina glides effortlessly to the music.

These two magnificent trees have shared this clearing for many years and are the best of friends.

One particularly bright sunny morning the great oak woke, stretched his branches and wiggled his roots. He turned to the willow tree and said, "Good morning Winifred, what a glorious day again in our great forest."

"Good morning Oscar," replied Winifred opening her eyes and stretching her wispy branches, "It is beautiful, isn't it?"

"You know I think today is a perfect day to stop and think as we look out over our fantastic forest that we live in!" said Oscar as he did his Tai Tree exercises.

"What a great idea!" replied Winifred as she shook her long branches, airing them in the morning summer breeze as she did her forest floor exercises, pulling in and holding for 3 seconds before releasing again.

Just then Winifred noticed something at the base of her trunk. There was something in between her roots that was not there yesterday, or at least she didn't think so.

As she swayed over to take a closer look she noticed a very small flower, trying to stretch as tall as it could to get some of the morning sunlight.

"Well I never," said Winifred in astonishment, "Look at that young flower trying to grow between my roots Oscar."

"By Jove so it is," Oscar replied just as shocked, "Hello little fella, what are you doing in our clearing?"

"Good morning great trees," said the young flower in a bright and bubbly way.

"My name is Sammy and I thought this would be the perfect place to grow up. I hope you don't mind?"

"Not at all," said Oscar in a fatherly voice puffing his chest out like a new dad would.

Over the next few months, the young sunflower grew stronger and stronger as Oscar, Winifred and Sammy became good friends, often talking about all sorts of things way into the summer evenings.

Oscar would try to teach Sammy all about the great forest, sharing his knowledge on how it became.

Winifred would give Sammy tips on growing, showing Sammy just how to shimmy his roots deep, deep down to get the best food.

"It's just like a dance," said Winifred as she elegantly swayed showing Sammy what to do, making it look so easy.

They all laughed as Sammy would try to shimmy his roots down but it did not look anything like Winifred's dance. "I can't dance and drink," said Sammy.

One particularly windy morning Winifred woke to see Sammy fighting against the wind. The wind was so strong it almost blew Sammy over. Winifred leaned forward allowing her long branches to shelter the little flower from the harsh cold winds.

Sammy looked exhausted, he had pods under his eyes and his petals looked all windswept and interesting.

"Thank you Winifred," said Sammy yawning and closed his eyes for a little well-earned sleep.

Winifred just smiled as she sheltered the flower while he slept a deep, deep sleep.

It had been a long hot summer. The birds had hatched their eggs and the sound of baby birds chirping for food filled the air. All was the way it should be in the great forest.

Sammy too had grown. Sammy now had bright yellow petals and a big brown centre with new shoots growing in new places. You could always see Sammy talking to the bees and playing with the birds long into the summer afternoons and their laughter filled the peaceful forest.

Winifred was very happy and content as she danced in the cool evening breeze and sang to Oscar.

One morning Winifred woke with a start. There was a chill in the air and a frost on the ground - the first cold snap of winter had arrived. Winifred swayed over to Oscar and said, "Morning Oscar, a bit chilly today isn't it?"

Oscar slowly opened his eyes rubbing them in an attempt to wake himself up, "Yes, summer is leaving us again for another year," he said wisely, closing his eyes again in an effort to get a few more minutes of peace and quiet.

Winifred leaned forward to say good morning to Sammy, only Sammy was not standing up straight like normal. Instead Sammy was lying on the ground. His eyes were still shut and petals droopy.

"Sammy, Sammy it is time to wake," Winifred whispered in Sammy's ear, but Sammy did not wake, in fact Sammy did not even move.

"Sammy, time to rise and shine," said Winifred softly swishing her long branches across Sammy's face to gently wake him, but he still did not move.

Oscar leaned forward looking intently at Sammy, "Oh dear," he said, "Oh dear, oh dear. It looks like Sammy too has left us," Oscar whispered to himself.

"What do you mean Oscar?" asked Winifred with a concerned look on her face as she scooped Sammy up in her branches bringing him closer to her, not really knowing what was going on.

Oscar sighed, "All living things come to fulfill their purpose and move on," said Oscar fighting back the sap from his weeping eyes.

Winifred shook her trunk, not wanting to believe Oscar.

"Will Sammy come back?" she asked.

"No, probably not to this forest," said Oscar.

"But Sammy was so young," said Winifred becoming angry at the thought of losing Sammy.

Oscar leaned over to Winifred placing his branches around her.

"Do you remember all those bees that played with Sammy? And all the birds that spent every evening playing and laughing in the fields with Sammy?" asked Oscar.

"Yes of course I do!" snapped Winifred.

"Well look out into our great forest and tell me what can you see," continued Oscar gesturing with his strong branches for Winifred to look.

Winifred slowly looked up from the ground. She looked and looked and looked harder. She started to see a few yellow flowers dotted on the ground in front of her. And as she looked harder still, she saw all over the forest floor a carpet of bright yellow flowers.

"That's right, Sammy may have only been with us for what seemed to be a very short time, but Sammy has left a mark on the whole forest," said Oscar proudly.

"Sammy's friends the birds and bees have spread sunflower seeds all over the great forest, as Sammy would have wanted," he said.

Winifred smiled. She knew Sammy would always be there with them brightening every day in his special way.

Barbara

Deep, deep down in the Amazon Jungle, where the trees are tall and the forest is dense, the sun is blocked by the leaves and all you can hear are the sounds of the jungle animals going about their daily business.

There is a family of young boa constrictors nestled in the safety of the hollow of a big ancient tree that towers high, high into the sky. There is Mum, Dad and Grandpa Boa who have lived there for generations.

There are also two young boas: Barbara Boa and Bob Boa. They are twins as they had been born at almost exactly the same time three months earlier. Actually, Bob was the oldest as he was born 28 seconds before Barbara.

Boa constrictors grow up very fast, they have to. They survive in a dangerous jungle with lions and tigers and the odd Gorilla who would stomp past early in the morning on their way to the watering hole for breakfast, not paying any attention to the family hidden in the tree.

As these two boa constrictors grew, they were fed well by their parents who wanted them to grow into big, strong, magnificent snakes - just as they had. So it was three square meals a day: two round ones, one short stumpy one and a long skinny one every second Thursday as a treat.

Bob Boa was a very happy and content snake. He loved his food, always looked fitter and leaner than Barbara, was the team leader at constriction classes and always had a current squeeze.

Barbara Boa was not so athletic. She could not get the grasp of constricting without constricting herself, wasn't as popular as her brother with the other snakes and was starting to see some lumps and bumps appearing in her physique that Bob just didn't have!

Her brother was continually shedding his skin…layer after layer… and would often do what boys do and leave their old skin lying around on the floor for their mum to pick up. This was a constant reminder to Barbara that she wasn't Bob.

Bob would produce new muscles each time he shed his skin. He did not have any resistance to this and in fact, it just made him more and more of an Amazon group idol.

Well Barbara Boa, she was intimidated by this and was a little scared to shed her old skin, not knowing what she would find. Her skin was tatty and did not really fit her too well anymore but she kept hold of it anyway, just in case.

Barbara told the other snakes she was suffering from water retention and it would go away, so leave her alone. They giggled at Barbara as she tried to slither away when another bulge appeared, tripping her over before she could get out of sight.

She slithered off to hide in the undergrowth to be on her own so the other boas would not see she was different. As she made her way through the dense undergrowth, she felt uncomfortable and just wanted to change the way she looked.

Barbara Boa was very upset. She would look at herself in the big pond, wondering to herself why she was not as strong, handsome and popular as her brother.

"I just want to be like Bob!" she screamed at the top of her voice.

Barbara began to cry. As her tears spilled out into the big pond making ripples, she heard a scurrying noise behind her back. She thought it was the other snakes coming to make fun of her, so she hid inside with her head in the centre of her coil.

She was startled when she heard a voice from behind her.

"You should try being a mouse! Everyone likes to eat mice around here - but no one asks you how you feel about that, do they?" squeaked the voice.

When Barbara looked around, she couldn't see anyone and wondered if she had actually heard the voice at all.

She decided to speak to the great boa who knew all: Grandpa Boa! She picked herself up and slithered off rather awkwardly to find him.

Grandpa Boa was easy to find as he did not go very far these days. He could always be found lying in the sun with his tail up in the air listening to the sports review on the Jungle Drum news.

Grandpa could see his granddaughter was upset and knew why. Grandparents know everything, you see.

Grandpa spoke to Barbara and told her that in order to become who she was destined to be she needed to accept the differences, allow the changes to happen and learn from them, as it's what's inside that makes you – you!

Barbara was a little confused at first, trying to replay the wise words of her Grandpa in her head repeatedly. Suddenly it all made sense to her; she knew what Grandpa had said was indeed wise.

Barbara jumped up and gave her Grandpa a big kiss, almost knocking his glasses off the end of his nose before slithering away as fast as she could.

She decided NOW was the time she was going to change. She went off and started by rubbing her nose on the smooth rock beside the big pond, creating a small tear in her skin.

Barbara could see underneath it was shiny and smooth. In fact, it appeared to be nice skin.

She got inquisitive and looked a little deeper, "That's right," she said to herself, "Look deeper and deeper inside." Yes, there was some pretty good skin in there.

She got excited and tore the last of her old restraints off to reveal this magnificent boa constrictor!

Barbara leaned over and looked in the big pond and what she saw looking back at her made her smile.

She was beautiful! She had accepted that she was not Bob. In fact, she liked the new Barbara Boa far more than she had ever thought possible!

She was Barbara the Boa and proud of it - and very soon Barbara was not short of a squeeze or two herself!

Cyril

High, high on the hill is the biggest oak tree you could ever imagine. From the top of this tall tree you can see the whole countryside, from its rolling meadows to its fields of lavender. The morning mist especially made it a beautiful, relaxing place to be.

Cyril Squirrel has always lived in the great oak tree from the day he was born. His parents and their parents have nested there for generations. They built the squirrel house themselves, adding to it as their family grew.

Cyril's home was right at the top of the great oak. If you climbed out on the left branch just outside his window you could see into the village and watch all the people go about their business, the children in the school playground and the postman delivering his letters.

If you climbed out on the right branch you could watch the farmer milk the cows, herd the sheep and drive his tractor.

The best view of all was if you climbed to the top! Up the top in the middle was the best view of the whole forest. The forest continued as far as the eye could see, a sea of green tree tops. Cyril was very lucky to have such a beautiful and strong family tree to live in.

Cyril's best friend is Betsy Barn Owl. Betsy lives in the farmer's barn two fields away from Cyril's tree. Almost every night Betsy Barn owl would come to visit Cyril on her way out to dinner with her family. They were very good friends and shared everything, Cyril trusted Betsy very much.

One particularly windy and stormy night as Cyril was storing his nuts for winter deep, deep down in the hollow of the great oak tree, Betsy arrived looking flustered and calling for Cyril. She flew into Cyril's house but couldn't find him, she flew to the top of the great oak but still couldn't find him. Then she remembered he would be in the hollow of the tree so she flew down, down, down as deep as she could as fast as she would dare.

"Cyril, Cyril," squawked Betsy, "You had best come with me to the farmer's barn as there is a storm coming this way. Can you hear it? Listen!" hooted Betsy as loud as she could over the noise of the wind.

Cyril listened. The wind was howling and blowing the branches from side to side, almost calmingly.

Cyril looked up from the hollow of the great family oak tree, he could see that Betsy was worried. Cyril followed Betsy to the farmer's barn, jumping over the wooden fence as the storm grew stronger. Betsy and Cyril made it to the barn just in time as the winds howled through the barn doors, blowing them open with a loud bang!

The hay was blown all around the barn spooking Samantha the Horse as the lightning lit up the sky and the barn.

Betsy and Cyril hid under a bale of hay listening to the commotion outside, not knowing what was going on.

Betsy and Cyril hid until the storm had passed, as storms always do.

The next morning when Betsy and Cyril woke, the storm was over and the sun was out again. The birds were singing and the sweet smell of lavender filled the air.

The farmyard was covered in pieces of brush, tables and chairs that had blown down into the farmer's yard during the storm and the farmer's bike was lying on the floor.

"It is a right mess," said Betsy holding her head with her wing, not knowing what to do first.

Cyril left the safety of the barn and headed home. Climbing back through the paddock he could see that the storm had been fierce.

Skiddy the scarecrow was lying face down in the cabbages and Mr and Mrs Hopper, the rabbits who live in the field, were out collecting what was left of their carrot crop and loading them into their barrow.

Cyril climbed over the farmer's wall and across the ground of the forest before returning home - only to find the great family oak tree had been struck by lightning during the storm.

The centre of the family tree was still smoldering as the smell of smoke filled the air. It's black charred centre looked almost destroyed. In fact, the great oak tree was split right down the middle with half leaning to the left and the other half leaning to the right.

If you looked at it in a certain way it almost looked like they were trying to get as far away from each other as they could.

Cyril's beautiful home was lying on the ground next to the tree with its windows smashed and the furniture all over the forest floor.

Cyril just stood there looking at what had happened to his family home. He felt like he was watching it from a distance, like it wasn't really happening to him.

Cyril was very upset, not knowing what to do. He felt very alone, almost lost. He didn't know if it was his fault. If he had been here, maybe it would have not happened. But Cyril knew deep, deep down that there was nothing he could have done and certainly it wasn't his fault at all.

He now had to think about the future, not the past as that cannot be changed. He knew he did not want to move as he loved the family tree and all the fond family memories they shared together there.

"I know," said Cyril excitedly, "I will have to choose one side of the tree to live in!" Cyril thought hard and then thought some more, not knowing which side was better.

Cyril closed his eyes, spun around and pointed! He picked the left side of the split tree to put his home on.

He climbed on to the left side and went straight to the top and placed his home as best he could. It was not the same as before, in fact it leaned a little to the left.

"Nevertheless, it will have to do," said Cyril to himself, "Besides, what other option do I have?"

That night Cyril could not sleep as he tossed and turned in his bed listening to the tree branches creaking and moaning in the breeze.

Cyril began thinking that he had been so unlucky to have had his home split in two and how unfair it was, "Why me?" he asked as he began to feel sorry for himself, before finally falling asleep.

Cyril had a terrible night's sleep, falling out of bed every time he turned over, finally resting his head on the wall and his feet on the bed.

The next day Cyril woke with a sore neck and not very happy about sleeping on the left side of the tree. He had spent most of the night on the floor listening to the trees moaning and groaning.

"There must be a better way," Cyril thought, "If I cannot be on the left side then I will move to the right side."

So he did. He moved his house to the other side of the great oak thinking that was the better side.

That very night, again Cyril could not sleep as his home leaned to the right and there were just as many moans and groans as the left side. Tossing and turning trying to get comfortable, Cyril fell out of bed with a thud!

Cyril got very annoyed and shouted at the tree "This is not fair!" he shouted, "Why did you have to split? This is my home too!" Cyril began to cry.

Betsy had not heard from Cyril since the big storm so she decided to fly over to visit him, not knowing what had happened to his family tree.

When Betsy arrived Cyril was packing his bags getting ready to leave the great oak and his problems behind. He had gathered up all his belongings ready to move to a new home.

"What are you doing?" asked Betsy, a little puzzled by Cyril's actions.

"I have to leave," said Cyril angrily, "I can't live on the left side of my home as it leans to the left and I can't live on the right side of my home as it leans to the right - and both sides continually moan and groan. So I have to find another tree that hasn't split, to live in. It is so unfair, why me?" Cyril dropped his bags and sat on the log before putting his head into his paws and he began to cry again.

Betsy could see Cyril was very upset and wasn't looking for the best solution to his problems - in fact he was just running away from them and getting angry.

"This is the perfect tree for you Cyril - it is your family tree," said Betsy as she placed her wing on Cyril's damaged family tree almost as if she was comforting it.

"You are just looking at this as though you could have controlled it. You couldn't control the split, however you can control your future," said Betsy, wanting Cyril to see that this was not all bad.

"Things may be a little different from now on but you do not have to choose or move away, just find the good in it."

"What do you mean?" asked Cyril feeling very confused, "I can't choose a side."

"And you shouldn't have to," said Betsy. She flew over to the log where Cyril was sitting and asked him not to leave until she returned as she had a great idea.

Cyril sat on the log outside his home and waited for Betsy to return. He did not know what she had in mind but trusted her to think of something.

When Betsy returned, tucked under her wing was a length of the farmer's wood that had blown down during the storm and some old string from the barn.

Betsy went to work placing the wood between the two halves of the great oak, resting the ends equally on both sides. She then placed Cyril's home in the middle, tying it all down nice and tight.

"There," said Betsy proud of her handy work, "You now have the best of both halves of the family oak tree.

"I think you are very lucky Cyril. You now have a better view of the village from the left side of the great oak, you can now see into my barn on the right side and an even better view of the whole forest from your home in the middle."

Cyril climbed into his new home in his old tree and realised Betsy was right! He could see right into the farmer's barn and he could see far off into the village and the magnificent forest felt even more beautiful from the porch of Cyril's home as the warm sun shone on him.

Cyril smiled. Instead of feeling unhappy about the great oak splitting Cyril now felt like the luckiest squirrel in the forest - he just needed to look at it in a different way.

Cyril and Betsy sat quietly with a cup of tea and watched the sunset from Cyril's new home in his old family tree.

Frederick

Frederick is a Freeway; but much more than just a Freeway. He is the main road between the town of Ayr in the north of the country and the town of Lungsdon, which is in the south. Both are very important towns.

Frederick has been carrying all the traffic between these two major towns for years. In fact, he is the only way the people of Ayr can get to Lungsdon.

Frederick is so proud of his job and his very important role that he takes great pride in ensuring nothing blocks this traffic lifeline.

He ensures all the people from Ayr get to Lungsdon without any problems everyday and then all the way home again every night before he rests.

In fact, Frederick is so good at his job that when there is a holiday or a special occasion and more people travel from Ayr to Lungsdon than normal, Frederick would expand his roads.

He does this by concentrating really hard, making them wider and wider so all the traffic can make it safely and without any congestion.

One day Frederick noticed that some sections of road were in need of repair. They had small lumps and bumps which were making it difficult for the traffic to flow freely. The roads were beginning to look old and a little tired.

"Hmm, this is not a good sign, I must get these mended straight away," said Frederick to himself determinedly.

Frederick decided he was going to tell the Head Roads Manager at Brainston that he needed some urgent work done, as it is his job to organise the repairs on all the roads.

Off Frederick went on his journey to speak with the Head Roads Manager who was a very important person and sometimes a little difficult to get through to.

When Frederick arrived in Brainston, the headquarters of all roads in Uington, he realised just how busy it is up there. Roads and tunnels weaved everywhere and people rushed with very important messages to and fro at great speed like flashes of light.

Frederick noticed a person who was calmly sitting looking out from an island in the middle at all the hustle and bustle and wandered over to him.

"Who is in charge?" asked Frederick.

"Why you are," answered the very calm observer.

"I mean, who controls the roads?" asked Frederick again trying to make himself a little clearer.

"Aren't you?" asked the observer again.

Frederick leaned over the desk, "Where do I find the answer to my road problem?"

"If you look up higher at the next level where all the important decisions are made, you will find what you are looking for," the observer said pointing in the direction of the next level entrance.

Frederick decided to move up to the next level in search of the decision maker... in search of an answer.

Finally, Frederick found the Head Roads Manager and told him that he needed to have some urgent work done on his old and tired sections of road as the traffic was starting to slow down during peak times making it difficult to move properly.

"The traffic from Ayr is at risk of being slowed down so much it may stop," said Frederick. He knew how very important it is that the road between Ayr and Lungsdon stays open at all times and at all costs, as it makes everything flow properly.

"Humm, no no Frederick," said the Head Roads Manager, "We can't have that, you must stay open. You are needed to get all that traffic from Ayr to Lungsdon every day and back again every night," he said with a concerned look on his face.

"We can't be shutting sections of your road down for repairs," he said wagging his fat finger at Frederick.

Frederick didn't know what to do. He was very upset and knew the road had to be fixed immediately. "But what about my tired roads?" he asked almost pleading with the manager.

The Head Roads Manager thought for a minute, "Frederick, you will just have to wait and make do until we can spare the time," he said making his final decision.

And with that off went the Head Roads Manager to concentrate on another very important job, not giving Frederick and his tired roads another thought.

This made Frederick very mad and he went home, telling himself under his breath just how important he really is.

Frederick decided to go back to his job, working harder and harder to get all the Ayr traffic to Lungsdon as quickly and safely as possible because … that is his job.

Frederick started to puff and pant as it was getting more and more difficult to get the people from Ayr to Lungsdon and back again on time. The roads were beginning to get congested and traffic beeped their horns as they grew angry at the blockages.

The section of tired road was slowing all the traffic down and creating a traffic jam. "What am I to do?" cried Frederick, "If I continue on like this my road will get more and more tired and who knows what will happen then?"

Just then Frederick had an idea, "I know! I will stop working altogether!" he said to himself, "That will show the Head Roads Manager and then maybe he will have my roads fixed." Fredrick smiled a cheeky smile.

That night Frederick went about plotting how he was going to stop working. He would slow the traffic right down until his roads were fixed by the Brainston Roads Manager. "It's not going to hurt anyone," thought Frederick, "I don't think?"

Frederick was pleased with his plan, "I had best get some sleep," he said, "I have a very big day tomorrow."

The next morning Frederick waited until all the traffic from Ayr started on their journey to Lungsdon. Then Frederick concentrated really hard… but this time instead of concentrating to expand his roads as he would normally do, he constricted them, making them much smaller. He constricted them so much that no traffic from Ayr could get through to Lungsdon at all. This created a major blockage!

With a big smile on his face Frederick thought to himself, "That will show the Head Roads Manager just how important I am."

Frederick, feeling very pleased with himself, sat back to enjoy the traffic jam that he had created. It wasn't long before Frederick could see that the town of Lungsdon had stopped working; the whole town had come to a complete stop! The normally busy town wasn't moving at all.

What Frederick didn't think about when he was plotting his big plan was that people needed to make Lungsdon work, were stuck at Ayr. Frederick had forgotten that Lungsdon needed Ayr to work properly.

Frederick became a little worried as he started to feel dizzy, "That's right," Frederick suddenly realised, "Lungsdon makes the energy that I need to power my roads from Ayr to Lungsdon. It not only powers my lights but the whole town of Brainston too."

Just then Carmen the Helicopter flew over Frederick's roads. She could see all the traffic from Ayr stuck just before Lungsdon. "What's wrong Frederick?" she asked, "The traffic isn't getting through to Lungsdon and Lungsdon has stopped working properly!"

"Well…my roads need fixing," said Frederick, "So I thought I would stop working until they were fixed.

"I thought if I stopped the traffic from Ayr getting to Lungsdon then the Head Roads Manager would have to fix my roads," he said as he held his head, trying to stop it spinning.

"But I'm not feeling very well now…" said Frederick breathlessly.

Carmen smiled, "Frederick, you know stopping the traffic from Ayr isn't going to help your roads get fixed. The road workers need to collect their trucks so they can mend your roads and their trucks are in Lungsdon charging up.

"Frederick…you need to relax for me…and concentrate right now. No, I mean really concentrate.

"You need to expand your roads…take a deep breath in and get all the Ayr traffic to Lungsdon.

"Now…close your eyes and slowly widen all your roads and feel the traffic flow, flowing right through to Lungsdon. That's right you can do it, it feels good doesn't it, moving all that traffic through the blockages.

"Carmen down, Carmen down, Carmen down," said Carmen quietly to herself as she landed next to Frederick, "Concentrate… only you can get Lungsdon working properly again, you know just how important you are."

"Ahhh…" said Frederick, "I feel the Ayr traffic flowing, flowing so smoothly it feels so much better. All the congestion and dizziness is going, going, gone… I can feel things moving along nicely now."

Just then the Head Roads Manager from Brainston arrived to see what all the fuss had been about. Frederick explained to him what he had done and why he thought he needed to do it.

The Head Roads Manager stopped and thought long and hard before replying, "Frederick, your roads are very important to us, so if we work together and ensure all the Ayr traffic makes it through to Lungsdon as smoothly as possible, then I will fix your tired roads for you straight away."

Frederick agreed, and as a special treat to himself Frederick concentrated really, really hard and expanded his roads even wider, allowing all the Ayr traffic to flow right down into Lungsdon with ease.

 Alfie

There is a small factory that sits nestled on the banks of a beautiful countryside river. It has lush green grass all around its grounds with trees and flowers which flow softly into the distance.

The factory has a driveway that winds left and right and left again as it turns from the main gates all the way deep down into the carpark.

When you reach the main entry, above the big wooden door is a sign, a big sign telling you this is Alfie the Battery Factory, complete with a big mat that says *Welcome - come on in.*

Way, way up high on Alfie's roof is a bird nest. It is neatly nestled in the corner of one side of the roof's guttering for shelter against the wind but with full morning sunshine. The nest belongs to Kenny, an elegant Kestrel with strong wings, magnificent feathers and perfect eyesight.

Kenny is often seen soaring high above the factory roof, higher and higher into the sky without a sound. You can hear the silence… he is like a whisper dancing on the fluffy white clouds before swooping down into Alfie's garden. He picks some of the brightest flowers and lays them gently on Alfie's windowsills. Kenny would do this every morning before anyone wakes.

Alfie is the only battery factory in the district. He makes all shapes and sizes of batteries for the local shops as we need all shapes and sizes to fill different needs.

The shops then sell the batteries to the local children for their remote control cars, torches, dolls and other toys. This makes Alfie a very happy factory as he can hear the children playing in the streets and in the school playground with the toys that Alfie's batteries power.

Every morning, just before the sun comes up and the mist on the ground is just beginning to rise, the trucks would arrive at Alfie's front doors delivering the fuel for Alfie to turn into energy for his batteries.

Alfie will only use the best, the cleanest and the healthiest fuel as Alfie loves his job. He knew children all over the local town used only his batteries to have fun, so only the best will do.

One bright summer's day as Alfie was working away making the energy out of the healthy clean fuel into batteries, Kenny landed on Alfie's roof.

"Alfie, have you noticed we have some new neighbours?"

"Who?" asked Alfie, very excited to hear of new friends to meet.

"There is a family of birds near the riverbank. I think they are Swans living amongst the reeds at the bottom of the factory grounds," said Kenny.

"Well, do you think we should invite them up for afternoon tea with us?" asked Alfie, "I mean, we should be friendly to all our neighbours, shouldn't we?"

"Great," answered Kenny very excitedly.

That afternoon Kenny launched himself off Alfie's roof, soaring higher and higher into the sky before swooping through the trees and flying down to the riverbank, making the flowers bow as he passed them at great speed.

Landing gracefully on the edge of the riverbank, Kenny knocked on the front door of the new family and invited them up for afternoon tea with him and Alfie that very afternoon.

Mr and Mrs Swan and their daughter Sally were delighted to be invited to join them. So they headed up over the lush green grass and into Alfie's front garden. Kenny Kestrel and Alfie made them feel very welcome and they soon became good friends over some tea and cake.

Kenny and Sally could be heard giggling and laughing as they played and chased around Alfie whilst Alfie showed Mr and Mrs Swan just how important his factory is.

Over the next few months Sally Swan would pop in for afternoon tea with Alfie and Kenny almost every day on her way home from school. She would always stop off and tell Alfie about her progress in diving classes. In fact, Sally was the best swan diver in her year making her father a very proud swan.

They would also talk about her beautiful new home on the banks of Alfie's river. Sally would talk about playing with all the ducks and the fish. The water is so clean and clear that she can happily swim late into the afternoon after doing her homework.

Alfie would show Sally how he turns fuel into energy and how he makes the different batteries, proudly boasting to Sally that it makes him very happy and the local children very happy too.

"If you listen… I mean really listen, you can hear children laughing and that always puts a big smile on our faces," said Kenny as he followed Sally around the factory listening to Alfie.

Kenny had heard Alfie's story hundreds of times but listened as intently as if it was the first.

Alfie was doing so well at making his batteries that one day Mr Niles Voltz, the Factory Manager, told Alfie that they were going to sell Alfie's batteries all over the world because they were the best batteries and had more energy than any other.

"That would make even more children laugh and be happy. That will make me very happy too," thought Alfie. In fact, Alfie was so happy he began to work harder instantly to produce more and more energy for more and more batteries.

"Full steam ahead," said Alfie not really thinking, just doing.

In order to do this

Alfie was having more fuel delivered sometimes two, three or even four times a day. Soon Mr Voltz had to extend Alfie's walls making him bigger and better so he could produce more and more energy.

One afternoon several weeks later Kenny flew in to see Alfie. "Have you seen Sally?" asked Kenny.

"No I haven't!" said Alfie, "I have been so busy, I haven't thought about her."

Kenny sighed. He was a little worried; it was not like Sally to stay away for so long.

Kenny decided to fly down to the riverbank and invite Sally up for tea and cake. It had been such a long time since Sally had visited and Alfie could do with the rest, he has been working so very hard.

So Kenny launched himself off Alfie's roof, again flying high, right up, up… so far up you really have to concentrate and squint your eyes to see him, before he glided down, down softly landing on the riverbank.

When Kenny arrived at Mr and Mrs Swan's house they told Kenny that Sally was very sick. In fact, she was in her nest and could not get up at all.

"What's wrong with Sally?" asked Kenny.

Mr and Mrs Swan did not know. They had asked all the wise owls but none of them knew. Kenny rushed back to Alfie to give him the sad news. "What can we do?" asked Kenny.

Alfie was very upset to hear that his friend was so sick. He wanted to help Sally. "I know, we must find out what is making Sally so sick and get her the right medicine," said Alfie.

Kenny and Alfie thought and thought. They were concentrating very hard, but still could not think why Sally was getting sick.

Kenny said he had noticed some of the fish and ducks were not swimming in the river anymore, maybe Sally was sad and upset that she had no friends to play with.

Alfie thought about this, "Kenny, could you go and ask the fish why they won't play with Sally. Maybe if they knew Sally was sad and she was sick they would come back."

Off Kenny flew. He soared high into the sky, so high you can see for miles. As Kenny glided on the wind he could see the winding river disappear into the distance.

Soon Kenny spotted Gloria Goldfish who was teaching all the little goldfish bobbing techniques. Kenny swooped down, landing on a log lying beside the river and asked Gloria why they had stopped playing with Sally Swan.

Gloria looked a little puzzled, "Sally isn't the reason we stopped playing there - it is the water! It is making the whole class sick," said Gloria. "It smells terrible down there and it's brown and murky, so I moved the school further up river to fresher, cleaner water," she said.

Kenny thanked Gloria and rushed back to Alfie with the news. "It's the river Alfie," said Kenny frantically as he landed with a thud on Alfie's windowsill, "It is making the fish sick, it smells and is brown and murky so the fish and ducks left!"

"But how?" asked Alfie, scratching his roof with his drainpipe. Alfie did not understand why the water was so smelly and brown down at the bottom of the grounds. He just hadn't thought of it before.

"We had better get Mr Voltz to test the water," said Alfie assertively. With that Alfie asked Mr Voltz to test the water to see what was making his friends sick.

When Mr Voltz returned with the test results he told Alfie the water is contaminated, dirty from your waste product.

"The waste from your factory is running into the river and making it smelly, brown and dirty which has made your friends sick," said Mr Voltz as he gazed at the dirty water in his test-tube.

"When you were small, the waste was controlled and collected in big white bags," explained Mr Voltz.

"Now you have grown and are a big factory the waste is too big for the white bags and is making the river smelly and sick," he went on.

Kenny thought, resting his chin on his long feathers, "So because you aren't disposing of your waste properly, it has also made the grass around the riverbank sick and go brown – it doesn't look very nice either," remarked Kenny as he peered over the back wall.

"What shall we do?" asked Alfie, realising he was making all his friends sick from the smelly brown water and waste.

"You can control the waste," said Kenny, "can't you?"

Alfie and Mr Voltz nodded in agreement with Kenny.

"That's it! Of course I can," said Alfie, "I will control my waste. I will stop it leaving the factory until we have it taken away in the proper chutes!"

"That's a great idea," said Mr Voltz, "You are big enough now to control it yourself... and I know you can do that, can't you?"

"It just takes some concentration and thought," added Kenny

Mr Voltz had also heard that people used the waste from factories and recycled it into plant food, helping the farmers once it had been collected and cleaned.

"So that is what I will do," decided Alfie with a big smile and a determined look on his face. And he did.

Alfie knows how to control the waste. Twice a day it is collected and taken away in the proper white chutes, just like all the other big factories.

At first Alfie had to really concentrate and remind himself to control the waste and to only let it go into the proper chutes. He made some mistakes at first, but after a little time he now controls his waste without even thinking about it.

"Controlling waste is easy, isn't it," said Kenny laughing as he flew past Alfie's windows.

Very soon the water was clean and clear, cleaner than it had ever been. The fish have come back to play in the beautiful water and it wasn't long before Sally was better and joining Alfie and Kenny every afternoon for tea and cake again.

George *and* Toby

In the sleepy town of Bedford lives Toby. Toby is a sheep farmer. His farm stretches through the whole length of the Bedford Valley from the pillowey white mountain peaks right down to the bottom of the soft fields below.

The whole valley is covered in a fluffy sheet of green grass and shady trees to shelter the sheep from the warm afternoon sun.

Toby has been a farmer all his life and loves his job and sheep more than anything else. His father was a farmer and also his grandfather before him. You see, Toby isn't any ordinary farmer. Toby keeps his sheep in the fields of the Bedford Valley during the day and lends them out each night to boys and girls who can't sleep.

Toby delivers ten sheep to each house where a child is still awake, so they can count the sheep jumping the fence outside their windows to help them to sleep. Most children only get to seven or eight sheep before falling into a sound sleep.

When all the boys and girls fall asleep… and you always do, the sheep wander off back to their paddock to join their friends. This is a very special service Farmer Toby offers because you couldn't imagine a world where there are no sheep to count and boys and girls who can't go to sleep!

At the top of the valley is a big dam where all the water for the day is stored. This dam has grown big and strong over the years, holding all the water the town needs and more.

When the town requires some water, the watchperson releases the big taps and lets just enough water flow into the areas where it is needed - any more and the Bedford Valley will flood, so the watchperson has a very important job of letting the right amount of water out - they are always very careful.

The watchperson needs to watch the water level and if there is too much, day or night, they must open the taps and let the water flow into a very special place called a catchment, a place where it won't flood Toby's farm and the sheep can stay safe and dry in the Bedford paddocks.

Day Watchperson Emma is new and wants to make a good impression on night Watchperson George. She wants to learn all she can from him, as he has been a watchperson for as long as she can remember. Everyone says George is the best watchperson there is.

Every night George starts work just as it gets dark. He would conduct his checks ensuring the watchperson's area has been cleaned, the windows have been washed and the steps brushed clean.

George would check the level of the dam to ensure there wasn't too much water in it. He would always let out as much water as was safe, just in case.

Windows washed	**check**
Steps brushed	**check**
Dam level checked	**check**
Taps opened	**check**
Taps closed	**check**
Handles cleaned.	**check**

… George would say to himself with his clip board under his arm. When George was happy everything was done he would let Emma go home to bed.

On Saturday it was George's birthday and Mrs Thinkaton had baked George a big chocolate birthday cake with thick chocolate icing and a lot of candles. She had delivered it to the watchperson's office at the top of the dam as a special surprise for George.

When George arrived for work he started his rounds. Just as he was going to do his first checks, he noticed the big chocolate cake sitting in the window.

"That looks a fine chocolate cake," he said to Emma as his mouth began to water. "Is that for me?" he asked, hoping she would say yes.

Emma smiled, "Yes it is George. Mrs Thinkaton dropped it off for your birthday, she said it was your surprise."

"It does look a very fine cake indeed, would you like to share some with me before you go home?" asked George, already cutting a large chunk for himself.

"Yes please George," answered Emma, quickly searching for some plates in the cupboard under the window.

George cut two very big pieces of chocolate cake, "One piece for Emma and one piece for George," he said with a chuckle.

Emma and George enjoyed Mrs Thinkaton's chocolate cake, tucking into it with a hot cup of tea.

"You had best be off," said George to Emma as he wiped the cake from his stubbly face, "Before it gets too late."

With that, Emma gave George a kiss on his cheek and wished him a very happy birthday, "See you in the morning," she said waving as she ran home.

"Maybe just one more piece of cake," said George to himself as he cut himself a very large piece and placed it on his plate. "This is the best chocolate cake I have ever tasted," he thought.

Farmer Toby was gathering his sheep in the paddock below the dam, ready for the sleepless boys and girls of Bedford. Just then Farmer Toby noticed some water coming very slowly down the valley.

It wasn't much at first but then it became deeper and deeper. The water was starting to rise up around the feet of the sheep, scaring them and they bleated aloud for help from Farmer Toby.

"That's odd," said Toby. "I wonder why there is water in Bedford Valley? There isn't supposed to be water in here. Maybe it's the dam?" thought Toby, worried about his sheep getting wet feet.

Toby decided to move his sheep to higher ground and check on where the water was coming from before everything got too wet.

Toby walked along the Bedford Valley all the way up to the dam, getting wetter feet as he climbed higher. He looked all around but could not see anything wrong with the dam or where the water was coming from. "This is not right," he thought as he scratched his head.

He was just about to walk away and look elsewhere when he noticed one of the overflow taps was open and water was flowing into the valley.

"That's odd," thought Toby, "That shouldn't be open at night. I had best check with the night watchperson."

Farmer Toby climbed up the side of the dam and as he walked into George's office he could see Watchperson George was still eating his chocolate cake.

"Hello Farmer Toby! Would you like some of my birthday cake?" George asked as he tried to wipe the chocolate from his face, "Mrs Thinkaton made it especially for my birthday and it's one of her best cakes ever."

"Not right now thank you George," said Toby keeping one eye on George and one eye on the lovely chocolate cake, "But I do think you should take a look at the water that is coming out of the overflow gates into the Bedford Valley."

"Really?" gasped George as he choked on a large lump of cake in his mouth.

"It has come all the way down to the sheep's paddock and my sheep have wet feet," said Toby.

George walked over to the dam wall, "That's odd," said George, "I didn't open that tap. I wonder why it is open now?"

Just then George noticed the water level gauge. It was way over the safe level. The tap had opened automatically because George had forgotten to let some water out before dark.

82

"Oh dear," said George as he slumped into his big comfy chair, "I forgot to check the dam levels tonight and one of the taps has opened."

George jumped up out of the comfy chair and rushed over to the control room to check all the dials, controls and gauges.

"I had better go and open the gate to let the water run off," shouted George as he ran past Toby.

George turned the big tap to the right. The tap stopped the water flowing into the Bedford Valley and directed it into the special white catchment area.

"I'm so very sorry Farmer Toby," said George removing his cap to scratch his head,

"I always make sure the dam isn't too full before dark. I must have forgotten tonight."

George washed his hands as he eyed off the last two pieces of chocolate cake still sitting on the table.

"Is there anything I can do to help you make up for your lost time?" asked George

"Actually there is," said Farmer Toby, "I have five children tonight who haven't gone to sleep yet. Would you be able to help me deliver the sheep to them?"

George smiled, "I would be glad to assist you," he said.

George and Farmer Toby turned off the taps and headed down the valley towards the sheep's paddock. When Farmer Toby and George arrived to collect the sheep, they were all huddled under a tree trying to keep their feet warm and dry. You see, if sheep get too wet, their wool starts to shrink.

Farmer Toby and George loaded the sheep into their trucks and off they went

delivering sheep to the five boys and girls of Bedford just in time to get them to sleep.

The next morning when Emma returned for her day shift, George told her what had happened the night before; because he had forgotten to open the gate before it got dark the water had flooded the Bedford Valley making all Farmer Toby's sheep's feet wet.

"You see," said George, "We all make mistakes from time to time, but it is very important that you always check the water levels before dark and ensure you have let as much water out into the white catchment area as you possibly can."

So the next time it gets dark make sure your dam is empty, we wouldn't want any sheep to get their feet wet, would we!